DISNEY'S

THE LITTLE MERMAID

NEFAZIA VISITS THE PALACE

by Suzanne Weyn

illustrations by Fred Marvin

DISNEY PRESS

NEW YORK

For Diana Weyn Gonzalez,
with great love

Produced by arrangement with Chardiet Unlimited, Inc.

Library of Congress Catalog Card Number: 92-53937

ISBN: 1-56282-247-0

FIRST EDITION

1 3 5 7 9 10 8 6 4 2

NEFAZIA VISITS THE PALACE

"Flounder, look!" cried the little mermaid princess Ariel. She was staring out her bedroom window at the line of colorful tropical fish, black-striped sea horses, and large conch-shell coaches that was approaching King Triton's underwater palace.

Ariel turned and swam out of her bedroom before her best friend, Flounder, could even say a word. She swam down the shimmering pearl-lined palace halls, her long red hair streaming behind her.

"Wait for me!" cried Flounder, hurrying to catch up.

Ariel and Flounder arrived in the palace courtyard as four of Ariel's older sisters rushed in from the other side. Aquata, the eldest of King Triton's daughters, hurried to straighten her pointed golden crown. "Who do you think is coming?" she asked.

"Father didn't say he was expecting anyone," said Alana, her dark spiral curls bobbing around her neck.

"Quick! Braid my hair!" Attina said to Andrina. "Maybe it's a handsome mer-prince."

"Maybe it's a fat old fluke of a duke," laughed Andrina as she braided Attina's light brown hair.

Just then Arista, another of Ariel's sisters, swam into the courtyard. "Did you see them? Did you see them?" she asked. "Gosh, they're so beautiful! So amazing!"

"You don't suppose she's talking about the striped sea horses, do you?" asked Attina, with a laugh. The sisters all knew how much Arista loved sea horses.

"Those are sea zebras. I've heard about them, but I've never ever seen one before," Arista said, twirling excitedly.

"Sea zebras come from the Indian Ocean," Andrina said. "That's an awfully long way off."

Adella popped her head out an upstairs window. "Did someone mention the Indian Ocean?" she asked as she brushed her dark, silky hair.

"Yes," Ariel told her. "We think whoever is coming to the palace might be from the Indian Ocean."

Still holding her brush, Adella swam down to join her sisters. "I heard there are black pearls in the Indian Ocean," she said. "I just adore black pearls. Maybe I can get a black pearl necklace from our visitor."

"Are new jewels all you ever think about?" Andrina scoffed.

"Excuse me for having good taste," Adella sniffed.

"Let's swim to the top of the wall and get a better look," suggested Ariel. The mermaids and Flounder followed her to the top of the coral wall surrounding the palace.

3

By now the parade had almost reached the castle wall. It was even grander up close than from a distance. The sea-zebra-drawn coaches were studded with bright jewels, and the sea zebras themselves wore headdresses of red fan coral. Even the brightly striped angelfish wore emerald rings around their tails.

"Someone should go tell Father," said Arista.

"Someone?" asked Adella. "Why not you?"

"Because I want to see the parade," Arista replied.

"Well, so do I," Adella shot back.

"Stop bickering," said Aquata, nodding her head toward the palace. "It looks like Father already knows."

King Triton, the ruler of all the ocean, stood in the palace entranceway, his long white beard wafting slightly in the gentle sea current. He wore his thick crown and carried his golden trident.

"Maybe we should get off the wall," said Alana. "Father doesn't like us to sit here. He doesn't think it's proper for princesses."

At that moment King Triton spied his

daughters. He smiled and waved to them.

"Well, what do you know," whispered a surprised Andrina as they all waved back.

"He sure is in a good mood today," Flounder observed. "He must be happy to see whoever's coming."

"We're about to find out who it is!" Ariel said excitedly. The lead coach was passing through the gate and into the courtyard. King Triton swam out to greet it personally. Flounder and the mermaids quickly swam down to join him.

"Who is it, Father?" Ariel asked.

"Why, it's . . . ," he began. But before he could finish, the door of the coach opened, and a beautiful merwoman appeared. She had piercing, deep purple eyes and long, luxurious blue-black hair that flowed weightlessly behind her. She was wrapped in several long shawls of bright see-through golden cloth, and she wore the most dazzling emerald gem on the top of her forehead.

"Nefazia!" Triton cried, his arms outstretched.

The merwoman took Triton's hands and smiled brightly. "How good to see you again,"

she said. Triton and Nefazia hugged warmly.

"Isn't she beautiful?" Ariel whispered.

"The beautifulest," Flounder sighed. "But not as beautiful as you, Ariel," he added loyally.

Ariel giggled. "You're sweet, Flounder."

Triton turned to his daughters. "Girls, I would like you to meet Nefazia. She's traveled all the way from the Indian Ocean just to visit. I've known Nefazia since I was a merboy. I lived with her family for two years while I was studying in that part of the world."

"It was a wonderful two years," said Nefazia, her voice low and rich. "Triton was such a mischievous merlad. And he was always dragging me into his schemes."

"Father? Mischievous?" Arista questioned. "What kinds of things did he do?"

"Well . . . ," Nefazia said, "I distinctly remember that my older sister was always trying to boss your father and me around. So, one day, Triton played a trick on her."

"What did he do?" Andrina asked eagerly.

Nefazia smiled. "My sister always wore her hair piled high on her head, held together by many hair combs. One morning Triton took away her basket of combs and replaced it with a basket of sand bugs."

"Oh! Yuck!" cried Adella.

"Yes, they are awful little things," Nefazia agreed. "My sister was so used to her basket of combs being there that she didn't even look. She just stuck her hand right in, and the bugs began to crawl on her arm. She jumped up so fast that the basket toppled over and the bugs went everywhere. I've never heard anyone scream louder. Triton and I were hiding in her closet. We tumbled out, laughing. It was weeks before my sister spoke to either of us. And for those weeks we were free from her bossy ways."

In all her life Ariel had never seen her father blush. But now a deep pink was gathering at his cheeks and temples.

"You must be tired from such a long journey," Triton said to Nefazia. "Come inside and rest."

Nefazia and Triton entered the palace while Nefazia's staff unloaded her coaches. Ariel and the others watched as mermen lifted trunks made of bright shells and mermaids carried glittering mother-of-pearl jewelry boxes.

"I'd better be getting home," Flounder said after the last coach had been emptied and the last box lifted.

"Okay, I'll swim with you to the gate," Ariel told him.

When Ariel returned, Aquata was sitting alone on a bench in front of the palace. "What's the matter?" Ariel asked. "Why aren't you inside with everyone else?"

Aquata shrugged. "Maybe it's nothing, but I have a bad feeling about Nefazia. She could be trouble. Big trouble."

Just then Arista swam out of the palace toward her two sisters. "Nefazia is going to let us ride her sea zebras!" she cried, tugging on Ariel's arm. "Hurry! I don't want to waste a minute!"

Ariel turned and swam off with Arista. Aquata sighed, then slowly followed her sisters.

That evening Ariel sat in the royal dining room listening to Nefazia tell more tales about the young Triton. Ariel barely touched her seaweed salad. She was much too interested in the stories to even think about eating.

"Now that's enough," Triton chuckled as Nefazia ended a story. "I don't want these girls thinking I was a rascal."

"Oh, but you were," said Nefazia. "But you were also charming, and you worked hard at your studies. Life seemed very dull after you left, although I *did* have adventures of my own."

"Tell us about some of them," Ariel urged her. "Please."

"Yes, yes! Tell us," her sisters chimed in. Only Aquata was silent. She listened quietly, her eyes darting back and forth between Nefazia and Triton. What was bothering Aquata? Ariel wondered.

"Would you like to hear about how I came to have those sea zebras?" Nefazia asked.

"Oh, yes!" cried Arista. "I thought no one had ever tamed one."

"These are the only tame ones I know of," Nefazia told her. "And I assure you, getting them wasn't easy."

"You mean you tamed them *yourself*?" Andrina said. "How did you do it?"

"Well, I found these sea zebras off the coast of Africa, not very far from my home," Nefazia began. "They were being attacked by killer whales. As you know, killer whales are not peaceful creatures. They attack dolphins, seals, and even other whales."

"They eat merpeople!" said Andrina.

"That's right," said Nefazia. "And sea zebras, too. I tricked the whales by blowing into a broken conch shell. The high-pitched squeals sounded like another pod of killer whales calling to them. The whales swam off and left the sea zebras alone."

"What did the sea zebras do after that?" asked Arista.

"The sea zebras were so grateful, they followed me everywhere, but they wouldn't let me ride them." Nefazia laughed at the memory. "I couldn't very well bring a herd of wild sea zebras home. So I had to tame them. I started by bringing them sweetened plankton cakes, which they love. . . ." Nefazia told them how, before long, she had tamed the wild sea zebras.

Triton and Nefazia continued to tell stories to each other, while the girls listened with pleasure, until late into the night.

Finally, Triton yawned. "Time for bed," he told his daughters.

"Oh, Father, I want to hear one more story," Ariel pleaded. She was enjoying herself too much to leave.

"Nefazia will be staying with us for a long

while," said Triton. "At least I hope so. You'll have plenty of time to hear more stories. Now, to bed."

The mermaids got up and kissed their father. "Good night, Nefazia," they called as they swam out the door. Only Aquata said nothing.

The sisters chattered happily on their way up to the royal bedchambers. As they swam down a hallway, a door opened, and a red crab with an important air about him scurried into the hall.

"What is all this racket?" Sebastian asked. He was the royal court composer, but he also tutored the princesses in their studies and often advised the King on matters of importance.

Ariel stopped, letting her sisters go ahead. "Hi, Sebastian. We were just talking about Father's guest. You would have met her if you'd come to dinner. Why weren't you there?"

"I was busy in the music room. I'm writing a new piece of music," Sebastian replied. "I lost track of the time."

"Well, you should have come," Ariel said.

"Nefazia tells the best stories."

Sebastian's eyes widened. "Nefazia is here? I haven't seen that wonderful merwoman in years." Without another word, he scrambled down the hall to the dining room.

Ariel swam up to the next floor toward her bedroom. When she passed Aquata's room, she saw that all her sisters were gathered inside.

"Of course she seems great now," Aquata was saying as Ariel entered. "She wants everyone to like her. But can't you tell why she's *really* here? It's so obvious!"

"Why?" Ariel asked.

"To marry Father, of course!" said Aquata.

The sisters gasped.

"Marry Father? Are you sure?" asked Alana.

Aquata wrinkled her nose and narrowed her eyes. "Oh, Triton, you were so brave and charming!" she said, scornfully imitating Nefazia. "Don't you think she was sweet to the point of sickness? And what about all that stuff she brought? Not to mention all her servants. Does it look like she's planning to leave anytime soon?"

"I wouldn't mind if she married Father," Ariel spoke up. "Why would that be so bad?"

"Ariel!" Aquata shot her a stern look. "Believe me, you don't want a stepmother. With a stepmother around you won't have nearly as much freedom as you have now."

"Why not?" Ariel questioned.

"Why not?" Aquata scoffed. "Stepmothers don't let you go off for hours on end. Nefazia won't just let you swim anywhere you want. She'll want to know every move you make. Your whole life will change!"

"Well, I like Nefazia!" Alana said.

"She's a phony," sniffed Aquata, straightening her crown. "Besides, I'm old enough to do anything a queen would do. I can run the palace. I can represent Father on some of his missions. With Nefazia here, I'll never get my chance."

"But she has such gorgeous clothes," sighed Adella. "She might let me borrow them."

"And her sea zebras are so lovely," added Arista. "I would love to keep them around."

"You won't see much of her clothes or her sea zebras once she catches Father," Aquata argued. "She cares only about herself. All she did was talk about herself all night."

"But we asked her to," Ariel reminded Aquata.

"And she did talk about Father," Andrina added.

"Of course she talked about Father," Aquata said. "Flattering Father is part of her scheme. I'm telling you, if she becomes our stepmother, everything will change around here. Do you really want that?"

The girls shook their heads uneasily.

Ariel was worried. If she couldn't swim about freely, then she could no longer explore the storm-torn ships that had fallen to the bottom of the sea. The wrecks were filled with things from the land above them, the land where humans lived, the land that Ariel dreamed of visiting someday.

Her father didn't understand how Ariel felt. He thought of humans as dangerous barbarians, and he had told Ariel to stay away from them and their things. So Ariel had her collection of human treasures hidden away in a secret grotto.

If she could no longer go to her grotto,

no longer explore the wrecks, Ariel thought, with sudden emotion—how could she possibly live?

"Listen to me," demanded Aquata, interrupting Ariel's thoughts. "If you want things to stay just as they are, we have to make sure Nefazia doesn't marry Father."

"But how do we do that?" asked Attina.

Aquata reached out and pushed her door shut. "I have a plan."

"Why do *I* have to do this?" Ariel protested. She was standing with Aquata at the doorway of the royal kitchen. King Triton had planned a fancy luncheon in Nefazia's honor, and the kitchen was filled with freshly prepared food for the occasion. The cook was nowhere in sight.

Aquata pressed a small red bottle into Ariel's hand. The label read Super Spicy Urchin Juice.

"You have to do it because you're always

poking around the kitchen and talking to Cook. It will seem natural for you to be here," Aquata explained. "Just look for the golden guest-of-honor plate and dump this stuff on the food." Aquata giggled. "I can't wait to see Nefazia's face when she swallows. This will make her food so hot that she'll turn red, cough, sputter, and look totally ridiculous in front of everyone! She might even be so embarrassed she'll leave right away."

"But maybe we shouldn't . . . ," Ariel began.

"I have to go greet the guests with Father," Aquata said, ignoring her. "He'll think it's strange if I'm not there."

"But . . . ," Ariel tried again. It was no use. Aquata was already off down the hall.

Ariel went into the kitchen. Plates of sea fruits had been set out on the counters, ready to be served. And just as Aquata had said, there was one golden plate.

Ariel uncorked the bottle as she went over to the golden plate. All her sisters had agreed that this was a brilliant plan, but Ariel wasn't so sure. She felt as sneaky as an eel and as low-down as a rockfish.

She sniffed the bottle opening. Her nose

19

tingled and her eyes hurt. "Whew!" she said, holding the bottle away from her.

Attina stuck her head into the kitchen. She quickly looked around to make sure Cook wasn't there. "All the guests have arrived," she whispered. "Did you do it?"

"Um . . . uh . . . I'm just about to," Ariel replied.

"Well, hurry up," said Attina, disappearing out the door again.

Ariel held the bottle over the food on Nefazia's plate, but then pulled it away. "I can't do this," she said softly to herself. "It's too mean." But she didn't want to let her sisters down. Once again, she raised her hand to pour. "No, I just can't," she said decidedly, recorking the bottle. This was just too rotten a thing to do.

Just then Ariel heard Cook and Sebastian coming up from the supply cellar. They were arguing loudly.

"It's not my fault if I don't have it," said Cook. "No one told me a guest was coming."

"You are supposed to stock *everything*!" Sebastian told him.

Ariel panicked. She put the spicy urchin sauce on a nearby shelf and hurried into the royal dining room. There was a low buzz as the merguests floated about, chatting.

Triton was talking to Nefazia when Ariel appeared. "Here she is," he said as he put his arm around his daughter. "We were wondering what became of you."

"Oh . . . I was . . . just around," Ariel stammered.

At that moment the royal sea horse messenger swam into the room. "Lunch is served," he announced in a squeaky voice.

The guests took their seats at the long banquet table. The kitchen door swung open, and a line of mermen in serving coats swam out holding trays of food. They set a plate before each guest. The special golden plate went to Nefazia, sitting at Triton's right.

"This looks delicious," Triton commented, unfolding his napkin. "We'll wait for the guest of honor to begin."

Ariel sat between Aquata and Adella. "This should be good," Aquata said with a mischievous grin.

"Aquata," Ariel whispered. "I have to tell you something. I—"

"Later," said Aquata quietly. "She's about to

take the first bite of her sea fruit."

With sidelong glances, the sisters watched Nefazia pick up a round piece of fruit. Adella grabbed Ariel's hand under the table. "I can't wait to see this," she giggled softly.

"But Adella, at the last minute I just . . ." Ariel tried to explain, but Adella wasn't listening. She squeezed Ariel's hand excitedly. "Here she goes."

Nefazia bit into the fruit and swallowed it. "This has a delightful tang to it," she said pleasantly.

"Tang?" Aquata gasped, glancing sharply at Ariel.

"That's what I was trying to tell you," Ariel whispered. "I didn't—"

Ariel didn't get to finish her sentence. The other guests had started to eat, and at once they began leaping from their seats, red faced and clutching their throats.

"I've been poisoned!" screamed the fat Countess Oystera.

Duke Dorselfin's eyes bulged in his head. "What is—is—this!" he sputtered.

Count Von Crableg began coughing so hard that his chair fell backward and his plate went

flying off the table.

"You spiced the wrong dishes!" Adella hissed at Ariel.

"But I didn't spice *any* dishes," Ariel whispered, completely bewildered by what was going on

"Cook!" Triton boomed. He had not yet bitten into his fruit. He rose to his full height, his fork still in his hand. "COOK!"

Cook burst through the kitchen door. "What's wrong, Your Majesty?" he asked frantically.

"That's what I'd like *you* to tell *me*!" Triton thundered.

Cook looked at the gasping guests. "I . . . have no idea," he said, horrified.

Sebastian suddenly hurried in. He took one look at the red-faced guests and immediately turned to race back out the door.

"Sebastian!" Triton asked. "What do you know about this?"

Sebastian slowly turned away from the door and scuttled from side to side. "Well, Your Majesty . . . ," Sebastian said breathlessly. "I know how Nefazia likes spicy foods. So I was trying to find something with a little zip to add to the meal. But Cook didn't have anything down in the supply cellar. Then I saw a bottle on the shelf that said Super Spicy Urchin Juice. I thought this might be just the thing to add some pizzazz to the lunch."

"You poured urchin juice on my sea fruit?" Cook screamed, aghast.

"Just a drop on each plate," Sebastian admitted nervously. "I didn't think it would be so . . ." He gulped. "So *strong.*"

"I *do* like my food spicy," Nefazia quickly said. "That's how we eat everything back home. Thank you for thinking of me, Sebastian. I'm just sorry if the food is too spicy for everyone else."

Sebastian brightened for a moment. But then he looked at the King, who was still glowering with anger. "Sebastian," Triton said. "Next time, check with Cook before you decide to play chef!"

"Yes, Your Majesty," said Sebastian, looking completely miserable.

"And Cook," Triton went on. "From now on prepare dishes that have a *little* spice to them. Sebastian should not have to fix your bland meals!"

"Yes, sire," said Cook with downcast eyes.

The lunch was quickly cleared away. New food was set out, but nobody felt much like eating. Ariel felt terrible.

Late that afternoon, after the guests had gone, Ariel lay draped across her bed. She was still thinking about the disastrous lunch when she heard Triton and Nefazia coming down the hall together. "Here's where the girls sleep," Ariel heard Triton say just outside her door. "Of course, all this will change—once it is yours to do what you wish with."

Change? Yours? Ariel froze. As Triton and Nefazia continued down the hallway, she got off her bed and swam over to the door so she could hear better.

"I'm counting on you to make everything different around here," Triton continued. "I hate to keep this from the girls, but we'll let them know when all our plans are settled."

"You are as sweet as ever, Triton," said Nefazia.

Ariel's jaw dropped. Aquata was right! Her father *was* going to marry Nefazia. And he *wanted* everything to change.

They couldn't let that happen!

Ariel smiled to herself as she swam away from the palace. It felt so good to be out in the vast, boundless ocean. It was delightfully quiet, too.

As she swam, she recalled Aquata's words. *Stepmothers don't let you go off for hours on end.* A shiver ran up Ariel's spine. Not be able to swim freely? The thought was too awful to consider.

Would Nefazia really be like that? Why would she want to stop Ariel from exploring when she'd had so many adventures herself? Perhaps she would think it was her duty as a stepmother.

King Triton spent so much time ruling the ocean that he gave his daughters a lot of freedom in their everyday activities. His daughters were used to being responsible for themselves.

"Hey, Ariel!" Flounder called out. He swam up alongside her. "How's your guest?"

Ariel told him all about the problem with Nefazia. "At first I didn't believe Aquata, but she was right. Yesterday I overheard Nefazia and Father, and it's all true," she said.

"Stepmothers aren't so bad," said Flounder.

"But change is out of the question," Ariel said firmly. "My life is fine the way it is."

"Well, don't think about it for now. I found something that will cheer you up," said Flounder. "Follow me."

In a flurry of bubbles, Flounder swam off with Ariel right beside him. They swam to a large ship that tilted to one side on the ocean floor. Its mast was cracked, and its side was torn open.

"We've already explored this one, Flounder," said Ariel.

"But we missed something," he replied. He darted inside the jagged opening in the ship's side. Ariel followed him in. The opening led them into a dark chamber. "Look at this," Flounder said. A shimmering glass ball with a flat bottom was nestled in a corner of the room.

Ariel carefully scooped up the object. Inside the glass ball were two tiny glass figures. They were humans, a man and a woman. "I found it this morning," Flounder explained. "I was just poking around."

"We must have gone right past it the first time," Ariel said as she peered curiously into the ball. The figures were perched on a tiny mirror. "I've never seen humans like this," she went on. "The woman is wearing something over her hands and on her head. And the man has something long and fuzzy wrapped around his neck."

Flounder floated near the ball. "Look what they're wearing on their—what are those things called that humans have where we have fins?" he asked.

Ariel bit her lip as she thought. What *were* those things called? "Legs. They're called legs," she remembered. "But I don't know what those things are at the bottoms of them."

"It looks like they're walking on water with little silver blades," Flounder observed.

"But they would fall through the water's surface. Could they be on ice?" asked Ariel, awestruck by the idea. "*Frozen* water, like the kind that floats around in the Arctic Ocean?"

"Has to be," agreed Flounder. "The silver things must be especially for walking on ice."

The ball tilted as Ariel looked at it, and small white flecks swirled around the figures. "Oh," gasped Ariel. "They must have sandstorms in the Arctic. Beautiful, glistening white sand."

Ariel held the ball to her heart. "What an amazing world it must be up there, Flounder. I have to get there someday. Let's take this back to my grotto."

From the outside, Ariel's grotto seemed to be just another cavern. But inside, behind the secret door, it was anything but plain.

At the top of the cavern was a small

opening that let in the gentle wavering rays of light from the top of the ocean. But the thing that made the place so amazing was its curved stone walls. The wafting sea currents had, over time, carved shelves into the walls. Ariel had crowded the shelves with the land treasures she'd collected. There were lamps, statues, silverware, jewelry, a telescope, a microscope, flags of many colors, and much more. Ariel wasn't sure what most of the things were. They were like pieces of a big puzzle to her. Somehow they all fit together and made sense in the remarkable world above the ocean.

"There," said Ariel, gently placing the ball on a shelf. "Now it has a place of honor!"

Flounder and Ariel spent the morning examining her treasures.

After a while Ariel said, "I have a music class this afternoon. I suppose I'd better get back."

As they slipped out the secret doorway, Ariel saw someone in the distance swimming toward them. It was a merwoman with long black hair.

"It's Nefazia!" Ariel said, pushing

Flounder back into the grotto. In a panic, Ariel crouched down next to him.

Ariel couldn't let Nefazia discover her grotto. If she did, she'd surely tell King Triton. Ariel knew that if her father learned of her collection he would make her get rid of it. He might even order it destroyed.

"What's she doing here?" Flounder whispered.

"I don't know," said Ariel. "I hope she isn't looking for me."

They watched as Nefazia hovered near the entrance to the grotto. But Nefazia didn't seem to be aware of them. With a push from her powerful tail, she began swimming straight up and away from them.

Ariel dared to stick her head out the doorway. She watched Nefazia swim until the sight of her shimmering tail was lost in the bright sunlight near the surface.

"How strange," Ariel murmured as she and Flounder floated out the doorway. "Where could she possibly be going?"

5

"Now, Princesses, try it again from the top," Sebastian said. Ariel and her sisters were in the middle of music class, practicing a new song.

Ariel slumped in her seat and sang the words, but her mind was elsewhere. She couldn't stop thinking about Nefazia. It had looked as if she were swimming to the surface. But all merpeople were forbidden to go above the water. What was going on?

Ariel wondered if she should tell her

sisters what she'd seen, but then she decided to wait until she found out something more.

"Ariel!" Sebastian's sharp voice snapped her to attention. "What kind of posture is that? Great singers do not hunch like humpback whales."

"Oh, sorry, Sebastian," Ariel murmured, straightening. "I guess my thoughts were somewhere else."

"When are they not?" Sebastian scoffed.

Just then Triton entered with Nefazia at his side. "Hello, Your Majesty," Sebastian said, hurrying to greet them. "And dear Nefazia, how are you this fine day?"

"Very well, Sebastian," Nefazia replied. "King Triton always boasts of how well you've tutored his daughters. I came to see one of your wonderful classes."

Red as his natural complexion was, Sebastian turned one shade redder. "You are too kind. Too kind!" he cried delightedly.

While Sebastian was talking to Triton and Nefazia, Andrina tapped Ariel's arm. "Aquata has another idea," she whispered.

Ariel joined her sisters as they tried to make a circle around Aquata without attracting Sebastian's attention. "You know that when we work at our singing, we sound great," Aquata whispered. They all knew this was true. The princesses were famous throughout the ocean for their rich, harmonious singing.

"So let's show Father what a croaking toad his little Nefazia is," Aquata went on.

"How?" asked Andrina.

"Leave it to me," Aquata replied. "Just sing your best."

"Girls, please!" Sebastian hissed in a low tone as he scurried over to them. "Do not embarrass me at this moment."

The mermaids floated back to their seats. "We would like to give a little performance for Nefazia," said Aquata sweetly. "Would that be all right, Father?"

Triton's chest puffed with pride. "That would be delightful. Sebastian, would you please call in the royal musicians?"

"Certainly, Your Majesty." Sebastian went to a giant pearl shell hanging on the wall. He hit it with his conductor's baton, and a sweet ringing filled the room. In seconds a group of sea creatures rushed in so quickly that they left a trail of small bubbles behind them. Three small fish with long, hornlike noses sat together. A starfish stood beside them, ready to play a xylophone made from seashells. Next to her, a giant squid sat behind a delicate harp.

"We would like to sing 'The Sirens' Song from the North Atlantic,'" Aquata announced.

Sebastian cringed. "Maybe you would like to try something else," he suggested. "Something, uh, a little less difficult, perhaps."

"No. That's exactly what we want to sing," Aquata insisted.

Poor Sebastian, thought Ariel. Aquata had selected the most difficult song they knew. Sometimes they still got confused in the middle of it. If they didn't get it right this time, Sebastian would be terribly ashamed.

"Is there a problem?" King Triton asked, sensing Sebastian's unease.

"Oh, *no*, Your Majesty," Sebastian said a bit too loud. "No problem at all."

Sebastian waved his baton, and the musicians began to play. The squid's many arms flew across the strings of the harp. The starfish spun up and down the length of the xylophone, and the three horned fish made the sounds of a rich brass melody.

It was the mermaids' turn to sing. Ariel sat up straight and paid close attention. She wanted Sebastian to be proud of them.

As Ariel sang, she watched Sebastian. Slowly the look of panic on his face melted and was replaced by one of fierce pride.

The sisters sang beautifully, more beautifully than ever before. Their tone had the crystal clearness of sound waves bouncing off an iceberg. According to an old legend, the beauty of "The Sirens' Song from the North Atlantic" had been known to make sea lions weep with joy. Ariel felt certain that this must be true.

"Bravo!" Nefazia cried when the song ended.

"Magnificent!" said Triton proudly.

Sebastian looked as if he were about to faint with happiness.

"Nefazia, would you sing us a song now?" Aquata asked, a hint of challenge in her voice.

Andrina leaned close to Ariel. "I'd like to see her beat that," she whispered.

"Oh, no, I couldn't," Nefazia protested.

"Yes! Please! We insist," the sisters spoke at once. "Come on, Nefazia. Oh, please sing!"

"Well, I . . . ," Nefazia said, uncertain. After a moment, she turned to Sebastian. "Do you happen to know 'The Song of the Bengal Tiger-Shark Herders'?"

"No, I am *so* sorry," Sebastian stammered. "That is a new one for me. I don't know how I missed it. I will learn it tomorrow. Tomorrow? No! No! By *tonight!*"

Nefazia laughed. "It's all right, Sebastian. Not many merfolk in these waters know it. Do you have a drum?" Sebastian hurried to a large closet and dragged out a tall drum.

"A drum," Arista snickered quietly. "This should be worth a laugh."

"Wait till Father hears this," Adella giggled. "The title alone sounds dreadful."

Nefazia sat with her shimmering tail wrapped around the drum. She closed her eyes and began beating on it. Suddenly she threw back her head and sang out an amazing sound.

Nefazia's voice gave Ariel goose bumps. It was a call that seemed to rise up from deep inside her. Nefazia quickly ran up and down the scales, hitting notes higher and lower than Ariel had ever heard. At times it sounded like three voices were singing at once!

Everyone in the room was spellbound. When the song ended, Triton applauded, then stood and wrapped Nefazia in a hug. "I remember that song from when I lived with your family," he said. "But I never heard anyone sing it so well."

"Thank you," Nefazia said, beaming.

Sebastian wore a dreamy look on his face. It was obvious that he, too, had now fallen in love with Nefazia. "You must teach me that song," he begged.

"Certainly," said Nefazia graciously. "We can start this evening." She got up and went with Triton to the door.

Aquata sat slumped in defeat, her head in her hands. "I don't exactly think we made her look bad," Ariel said.

Arista looked at Aquata with a glum expression. "Any more bright ideas, genius?"

6

It was early in the evening when Ariel decided to go for a swim outside the palace grounds. She left her sisters whispering together in Aquata's room. They were desperately trying to devise a new plan that would make Nefazia so unhappy she would want to leave.

As Ariel passed the music room, she peeked in and saw Sebastian and Nefazia inside. Sebastian's head was thrown back, and he was warbling at the top of his lungs.

He was trying to learn "The Song of the Bengal Tiger-Shark Herders."

Nefazia pushed back her thick blue-black hair. "Perhaps with a little more practice, Sebastian," she said kindly.

Ariel swam on until she was outdoors. She loved this time of day. The sea plants waved calmly back and forth, and the sand shifted lazily with the gently changing currents.

Ariel floated with her eyes closed and let the current carry her along. She imagined she was leaping above the surface, feeling the warm sunshine on her skin and scales—that she was seeing the world above the ocean.

Dreamily, Ariel opened her eyes. A shadow was passing above her. She blinked hard, coming back to reality.

It was Nefazia! She was swimming far above Ariel, making her way through the water toward the soft light on the surface.

Ariel decided to follow her. As she swam, her imagination ran wild. Was Nefazia having a secret meeting with someone? Was she working with Ursula, the dreaded Sea Witch? Ariel had a horrible thought—maybe Nefazia *was* Ursula in disguise! Ariel had heard that the awful witch had the power to change her form.

Ariel gasped when she saw Nefazia break through the water's surface.

Did she dare to follow?

I have to, Ariel decided. No merperson was allowed above the sea. Nefazia was doing something forbidden, and Ariel had to find out why.

Ariel pushed up through the water's surface and squinted into the setting sun. Even its soft rays were stronger light than she was used to, and for a few seconds, she couldn't see. Oh, this world was so strange!

After a moment, she looked around. Where was Nefazia? Ariel caught sight of her swimming toward a boulder that jutted above the surface.

Then Ariel noticed a large ship sailing in the nearby waters. She had never before seen a ship that hadn't been destroyed by the storms that stirred up the sea.

Suddenly a lovely sound filled the air. Ariel turned toward it. Nefazia was sitting on the rock, singing. Her song was low and sweet, like a mermother crooning to her baby. In the pinkish sunlight, her tail

sparkled as though it were made of jewels.

Nefazia was leaning forward, looking at something. Ariel followed her gaze. Nefazia's purple eyes were fixed on the large ship.

Slowly the ship began to turn toward Nefazia. Ariel realized that she was luring it to her with her hypnotic song!

Ariel's mind flooded with stories she'd heard as a child, stories about a few evil merwomen who had lived long ago. They had magical voices and sang songs to lure ships into the rocks. The ships would crash, and dozens of sailors would drown.

The evil merwomen had been banished for their deeds. It was said that there were no more of them left. But maybe that wasn't true. Maybe Nefazia was one of them.

Ariel had to stop her.

She dipped back under the water and swam toward Nefazia. As she neared the rock, she saw that it was the tip of an underwater mountain. The mountain had many smaller jagged peaks hidden under the water. The ship's bottom would be torn out before it even reached Nefazia.

Ariel was frantic with worry. She popped

her head up and saw that the ship was closer than she'd expected. But Ariel was still far from Nefazia. Could she stop her in time?

The sailors crowded along the rails of the ship, trying to look at Nefazia. For a moment, Ariel was distracted from her mission. The sailors didn't look so different from mermen. Three of them climbed up onto the mast. Ariel watched them bend their legs as they climbed. How odd legs looked, she thought.

Nefazia continued to sing, luring the ship closer and closer.

Ariel dove again. This time she came up right behind Nefazia. In another minute, the ship would be dashed upon the rocks.

Reaching out, Ariel pulled herself up onto the rock. But before she could make another move, Nefazia's song changed.

"Go back. Turn back. Turn your ship around! Forget me. Forget me. I am but a dream! A dream. A dream. A mermaid is but a dream."

The ship's bow began to turn. One by one, the sailors left the side of the ship. The ones on the mast climbed down slowly.

Nefazia repeated her hypnotic song, stopping only when the ship was back on its course.

Ariel was about to slip quietly back into the water. But, without turning, Nefazia suddenly spoke. "So, Ariel, what do you think of these land creatures?"

"They're beautiful," Ariel replied.

Nefazia turned. She smiled softly at Ariel. "I think so, too. I've always wanted to see what they looked like in this part of the world. Now I know they are not so very different than where I come from."

"You mean . . . you mean . . . you go to the surface often?" Ariel gasped.

Nefazia raised her finger to her lips. "Don't tell anyone," she said with a mischievous twinkle in her eye. But then she suddenly grew serious. "You know it's forbidden, and with good reason. If humans caught you, they would study you and poke at you. They would never let you go. You must be very cautious around them."

"Yet you love to see them," Ariel pressed.

Nefazia nodded. "There is something amazing and poetic about the land and its creatures. Of all the remarkable things I have seen, the world above the sea is the most astounding. Can you understand how I feel? Most merpeople can't."

"Yes," said Ariel excitedly. "I do understand."

"Somehow, I knew you would," Nefazia replied.

Ariel was suddenly seized with a bold impulse. "Come with me," she said. "I want to show you something."

This is crazy, thought Ariel. What if she tells Father? But she kept going. She swam straight to her treasure grotto with Nefazia by her side.

"What is this?" asked Nefazia as she followed Ariel through the secret doorway. Then she drew in a sharp breath. "Oh my!" she gasped, looking around at Ariel's collection.

"It's a secret," said Ariel. "No one besides my friend Flounder knows about it."

Tenderly, Nefazia picked up the glass ball. She shook it. "Snow," she murmured.

"Snow?" Ariel questioned. "I thought it was sand."

"It's snow. I saw it years ago during a trip to the very southernmost tip of the Indian Ocean. It is unbelievably cold there."

"Did you see these humans with silver things at the bottom of their legs?" Ariel asked.

"No. I saw seals and penguins. I didn't see any humans at all."

Ariel listened eagerly as Nefazia described the snow. "It must be beautiful," she said, hoping to see it for herself someday. Then she showed Nefazia the rest of her treasures.

"I want to find out what all these things are," Ariel said. "And someday, I'd like to visit the land."

"That may never be possible," said Nefazia. "When I was a girl, I myself dreamed of visiting the land. But I never have."

"There just has to be a way," Ariel insisted.

"Don't set your heart on it," Nefazia warned. Then she added, "You know that your father would be angry if he knew about your collection. Very angry."

Ariel nodded. "You won't tell him, will you?"

"No," said Nefazia. "I don't think he would understand why I went to the surface, either."

"I wish he felt differently," Ariel said.

"He makes his rules to protect the entire kingdom," said Nefazia. "As long as humans can't prove we exist, they won't come looking for us. Humans are very smart, and they would find a way to get down under the water if they thought we were real."

"That would be wonderful!" cried Ariel.

"Maybe not," said Nefazia. "Sometimes humans are like merchildren. They take things apart just to see how they work. And they can't always put the things back together again."

"Teach me your song," Ariel pleaded. "The one you sang just now."

"You're too young," said Nefazia. "There are too many things that can go wrong. I once saw a mermaid sing the song before she was old enough to control it. She accidentally lured a pod of porpoises onto the shore and didn't know how to send them back. It was a great tragedy."

"That's terrible," said Ariel, horrified.

"When you are older, I promise I will teach it to you."

Ariel was so happy, she threw her arms around Nefazia. "Oh, thank you!" she said.

As they hugged, Ariel realized that she liked Nefazia very much. In fact, having her for a stepmother would be great. She was so understanding and knew so many things. Aquata and the others had been wrong. She would let them know that as soon as she got home.

"My," said Nefazia, gazing up at the opening in the grotto. "Look how dark it's grown. We'd better hurry back to the palace."

"What a lovely collection," Nefazia said as they began the trip home. "Guard it carefully."

They swam quickly toward the palace. As they approached they saw King Triton himself waiting in front with a worried look on his face.

"Where have you two been?" he asked, his

brows knit together in concern. "We have been waiting for you for dinner."

"Do forgive us, Triton," said Nefazia. "It is all my fault. Ariel was showing me the sights, and the time simply got away from us. I apologize for being so late."

Triton's face softened, as it always did around Nefazia. "As long as you and Ariel are safe," he said.

"We had the best time," Ariel spoke sincerely.

"I'm glad," Triton replied. "Now, Ariel, please go upstairs and tell your sisters that dinner is served."

"I'd be glad to, Father," said Ariel, swimming up to give her father a peck on the cheek.

As Ariel swam away, she heard her father say to Nefazia: "Ariel seems to have grown quite fond of you."

"She's a fine, spirited mergirl," Nefazia replied.

No, Nefazia would not stop her from exploring, Ariel was sure.

Ariel found her sisters in Arista's room. "This will work, without a doubt," Adella was saying when she entered.

"Ariel!" Aquata scolded. "Where did you disappear to?"

"Oh, here and there," Ariel said.

"That's what you always say," Arista chided.

"Listen! I have to tell you something important," said Ariel. "I had a long talk with Nefazia. She's not at all what we thought. She'd be a *wonderful* stepmother!"

Aquata rolled her eyes. "That's just like Nefazia," she said. "She gets hold of the youngest one and butters her up."

"She didn't butter me up," Ariel insisted. "I simply got to know her."

"Ariel may have a point," said Attina. "We haven't really given Nefazia a chance."

"Don't you understand?" Aquata said. "If we *do* give her a chance, it will be too late. She'll be married to Father and there will be no getting rid of her then!"

"But maybe we won't want to get rid of her," said Alana.

"Believe me. I'm the oldest. I know. You will definitely want to get rid of her," Aquata insisted.

"I'm with Aquata," said Arista. "And besides, we don't want to waste this great plan we've come up with."

"Absolutely not," agreed Adella.

"What's the plan?" asked Ariel.

"I don't think we should tell you," said Aquata. "You're not on our side anymore."

"We'll just say that it's going to happen soon," Arista taunted her sister. "Very, very soon."

8

"Good-bye, Father," the sisters sang out. They were all gathered together in the courtyard the next morning. Triton waved back as he climbed into his gold sea-horse-drawn chariot. He looked up at Nefazia, who had come out onto her bedroom balcony, and blew her a kiss. Then he drove off with a procession of staff members following closely behind.

Ariel turned in time to see Nefazia waving back to him. Oh, why did Father pick today to talk with the octopuses about keeping their arms under control? she fretted. She had a feeling that Nefazia might need him.

"At least they had a chance to say good-bye," said Andrina quietly as they watched their father ride off.

"Oh, stop worrying about her," snapped Aquata.

"But your plan does seem awfully mean," said Andrina. "I don't like it."

"Let's call it off," pleaded Alana. "There's still time."

Aquata looked up to the balcony. Nefazia had gone inside. "There isn't any going back," she said. "I just pushed the letter under Nefazia's door. She's probably reading it right now. Father's leaving made everything perfect."

"What letter?" Ariel wanted to know. "Tell me."

"No," said Arista snippily as she followed Aquata and Adella back inside.

"Sorry, Ariel," said Attina. "Aquata said we can't tell you. And it's probably for the best."

Ariel put her hands on her hips. If her sisters wouldn't tell her what was going on, then she would simply stay near Nefazia all day. If anything at all happened, she would be there to help.

With her jaw set in a determined line, Ariel swam into the palace. She was on her way up to Nefazia's room when Nefazia came swimming down the hall at full speed. She swam right past Ariel.

"Nefazia! Wait!" Ariel cried. "Where are you going?"

"Oh . . . good-bye, dear Ariel!" Nefazia cried over her shoulder. "I can't stop to explain. I left your father a note in my room."

"But Nefazia!" Ariel called. "You can't just leave."

The merwoman didn't hear her. She was already racing away. Ariel swam after her, but she was no match for Nefazia's speed.

"What have they done?" Ariel muttered. She turned and swam up to Nefazia's room. She picked up the note fluttering on the soft shell bed. "Dear Triton," she read, "this morning, right after you left, I received an awful note from home. My sister, Defazian, is gravely ill. The letter was dated five days earlier! Darn that slow sea pony express! There is no time to lose—I must rush to her. Please inform my staff and tell them to return as soon as they can. I will travel more quickly without them. Thank you for your generous hospitality. With love, Nefazia."

Suddenly a hand reached out and snatched the letter from Ariel's fingers. "I'll take that," said Aquata. She quickly tore the letter to pieces and set another one in its place on the bed.

"Let me see that," said Ariel, grabbing up the new letter.

"Triton," she read, "I can't stand another moment in this palace. You and your bratty daughters are driving me mad! I could never marry you and live in this awful place. I wish never to hear from you again. Nefazia."

"Nefazia's sister isn't sick!" gasped Ariel. "*You* wrote the letter to Nefazia."

"That's right," said Andrina, coming into the room with the rest of the mermaids. "We had to get rid of her. The letter worked, didn't it?"

"Father will find out what you've done," Ariel pointed out.

"I don't think so," Aquata replied. "I don't think Father will ever speak to Nefazia again after he gets this note."

"But this will hurt him terribly!" said Ariel.

"It's better than letting him marry that awful merwoman," said Arista.

"She's not awful!" Ariel shouted. "Why can't you see that?"

"I think we went too far," said Adella. "Let's at least leave Nefazia's real letter."

Aquata looked down at the bits of the letter she'd tossed to the floor. "Impossible," she said. "Besides, if we don't leave a mean letter, then Father will contact Nefazia, and he'll find out what we've done."

"We have to stick with the plan the way it is," said Arista. "If we don't, we'll all be in big trouble."

"I can't believe you could be this cruel," said Ariel. "What you've done is terrible."

"It *is* terrible," Alana agreed softly. "I feel so guilty."

"So do I," Attina admitted.

"Oh, stop whining!" said Arista. "We just sent her home. It's not like we hurt her or sent her somewhere dangerous."

At that moment Sebastian scurried into the room, his sharp claws tapping along the floor. "Oh, there you are, Princesses," he said breathlessly. "And all together. That's good."

"What's wrong, Sebastian?" Ariel asked.

"I'm glad you're not outside swimming around. Your father just sent back word with the royal sea horse messenger. There's a pod of whales passing nearby."

"So?" sniffed Adella. "Whales don't hurt anybody. They eat seaweed and stuff."

"These are *killer* whales, child," Sebastian lectured. "They don't eat seaweed They feast on seals, sea lions, dolphins—and merfolk!"

Adella turned pale. "Oh," she gulped.

"Nobody is to leave this palace until I tell them to," Sebastian continued. "That is King Triton's order."

"Oh my gosh!" Ariel gasped. "Nefazia is out there. She may run right into those whales!"

"I never really meant to harm her," cried Aquata, suddenly frightened.

"We have to warn her," said Ariel.

"Nobody is leaving this palace!" Sebastian shouted.

But in a flash, Ariel and her sisters were racing down the hallway.

9

"I see her," Ariel cried, swimming ahead of her sisters. But Nefazia was still too far ahead for them to call to her.

"You mergirls come back to the palace this instant!" yelled Sebastian, who was paddling madly to catch up with the mermaids.

"We can't, Sebastian," Attina called over her shoulder. "We've done an awful thing, and we have to make it right."

"Will somebody *please* tell me what is going on?" Sebastian fumed.

"Look!" shouted Ariel. "She's resting on that rock. This is our chance to catch up with her."

Churning the water behind them, the sisters raced toward the rock. Just as Nefazia was about to resume her journey, Ariel cried out to her. "Nefazia!"

Slowly, as though she wasn't sure whether she'd heard someone calling, Nefazia turned.

"Wait!" Ariel cried.

"Wait! Please wait!" the mermaids called.

Wringing her hands, Nefazia waited for them to catch up to her. "What is it, girls?" she asked when they were near. "I'm sorry I didn't say good-bye properly, but I really must—"

"Your sister isn't sick," Aquata blurted out.

"What?" asked Nefazia. "But I got a letter saying—"

"We wrote it," Aquata confessed. "Actually, *I* wrote it."

"But we all knew about it," Andrina added. "All of us but Ariel."

"Why?" Nefazia asked with a shocked look on her face.

"Excuse me," Sebastian said breathlessly as he finally caught up with the group. "This is no time to be chitchatting. You can talk back at the palace. We don't want to float around acting like food for a pod of—"

At that moment the sparkling water turned black. All eyes looked up.

"—killer whales," Sebastian finished, with a fearful gulp.

Above them, five huge black-and-white killer whales silently sailed by. The silence was occasionally broken by sharp clicks and squeals as the whales spoke to one another in their special language.

"Shhh," Nefazia said in a whisper. "Get down slowly and don't move. Go *very* slowly—and don't make a *sound.*"

The sisters and Sebastian did as Nefazia said. With their heads down, they lay flat and motionless. Ariel didn't dare to look up.

After what seemed like a long time, the pod began to move on. "We did it," cried Arista, lifting her head.

"Shhh!" Nefazia hissed. But it was too late.

The last whale in the pod turned its huge head. With a whoosh of water, it began to swim down in their direction.

"Let's get out of here," screamed Adella.

The group swam frantically, but the whale gained on them quickly. This is useless, thought Ariel with terror as she swam with all her might. We can't outswim a killer whale! Turning, she saw that Arista and Adella were falling behind the others. The whale had its sights set on them. It would be a matter of minutes before it reached them!

Nefazia had seen this, too. Turning abruptly, she began swimming back toward the whale.

"What is she doing?" cried Andrina.

She's sacrificing herself, thought Ariel. Nefazia swam a zigzag pattern, drawing the whale this way and that, pulling its attention away from the others.

"She needs help," Ariel shouted.

"Ariel! Wait!" cried Sebastian.

But Ariel couldn't wait. She couldn't stand by and let Nefazia take on the deadly whale all alone.

In seconds, the whale spotted Ariel. It left Nefazia and began to chase her. Ariel ducked and tried swimming under its belly. Using its huge tail, it swooshed hard. Ariel was knocked around by the forceful current. The next thing

she knew, the whale was beginning to come at her again.

In a flash, she darted out of the way. Where was Nefazia? Ariel spotted her at the bottom of the ocean, smashing the tip of a conch shell on a rock.

Nefazia looked up at the whale. Ariel again tried to stay under the whale's belly as Nefazia swam toward her holding the shell.

Just as Nefazia reached Ariel, the killer whale began to roll. It seemed to know they were underneath it. The water began to swirl around violently. "Nefazia!" Ariel screamed as the merwoman was carried away from her by the churning waters.

As she yelled, one of the whale's huge fins slammed into Nefazia, throwing her to the ocean floor. Ariel, too, was pushed down by the strong currents. As she struggled to steady herself, she saw Nefazia lying motionless behind a huge rock. Ariel realized that Nefazia was unconscious. Beside her lay the conch shell.

Suddenly Ariel remembered Nefazia's story about the sea zebras and the killer whales. She had to get that shell!

"Ariel!" her sisters screamed.

She looked up sharply. The killer whale was coming straight for her.

Ariel swam desperately toward the shell. She hid herself behind the rock as best she could, put the opening of the conch shell made by the broken tip to her lips, and blew with all her might.

A high-pitched squeaking sound pierced the water.

Ariel blew again—even harder this time.

The whale stopped immediately and seemed to listen. It thought its pod was calling to it, telling it not to lag behind. It suddenly turned and quickly swam off.

Ariel kept blowing into the shell. She didn't stop blowing until the killer whale was far away.

A gentle hand touched her shoulder. Nefazia was floating beside her. "You did it perfectly, Ariel. Perfectly," she said quietly but proudly.

Within minutes, Sebastian and the mermaids clustered around, hugging Ariel. "I'm so sorry, Nefazia," Aquata sobbed miserably. "When I think I could have gotten you killed. And Ariel, too."

"I'm still quite confused," said Nefazia. "Why did you do this?"

"We didn't want you to marry Father," said Alana, tears in her eyes. "We thought you wouldn't let us do as we liked anymore."

"Marry your father? You silly mergirls," Nefazia said. "Your father and I have no plans to marry. None at all! I think of Triton as a brother, and he thinks of me as a sister. We're certainly not in love."

The mermaids were stunned. Even Ariel was confused. "But I heard you talking," she said. "Father said you'd make changes. And that he'd tell us when the plans were set."

Nefazia threw back her head and laughed. "Wait until I tell this to Triton."

"Tell Triton what?" a voice boomed behind them.

"Father!" Aquata gasped. "What are you doing here?"

"I might ask you all the same question!" Triton thundered. "Didn't I give orders for everyone to stay inside?" At that moment he caught sight of Sebastian. *"Didn't I?"* he asked the trembling crab.

"You see, Your Majesty," Sebastian began

nervously. "It's like this . . . Uhhh . . ."

"I can explain," Nefazia said. "I didn't hear about the whale warning. I was out, and the girls came to tell me. It was very brave of them, don't you think?"

The storm clouds lifted from Triton's face. "Yes. It was quite brave indeed."

"Ariel was especially brave," added Andrina.

"Oh, yes. She was wonderful," said Attina. "You should have seen the brilliant thing she did with a conch shell."

Together the mermaids clustered around Triton and Nefazia. Speaking all at once, they told Triton what had happened.

"But Father," said Ariel. "Why are *you* here?"

"My meeting ended quickly. The octopuses were very agreeable." Then Triton smiled. "Nefazia, your packages have arrived from the Indian Ocean," he said. "I was told of them when I returned to the palace."

"What packages?" asked Adella as the group began the journey home.

"You'll see," Triton said. "It's a little surprise Nefazia and I have been working on."

10

"Oh my gosh!" Ariel cried. Nefazia's servants were working all up and down the bedchamber hallway. They carried out old headboards and dressers and floated in with bundles of beautiful fabric, vanities made of glossy purple and pink abalone shells, and all sorts of exotic fixings.

"Look at this!" cried Adella gleefully. In her room, servants were hanging curtains beaded with tiny black pearls.

"Oh, I love it!" shouted Aquata from her

doorway. Artists were dipping sea sponges into colored squid ink and pressing lovely designs on her walls.

"A sea zebra mural!" Arista squealed with delight when she entered her room.

"This is the real reason I came," Nefazia told Ariel. "Your father wanted my help in redecorating your bedrooms."

"We certainly wanted them redone," said Attina, swimming by. "But we didn't think Father had noticed."

Nefazia smiled. "Your father notices more than you think. He knows that you are growing up and that you need rooms more suitable for young ladies of a royal household."

"Are *these* the changes you were talking about?" asked Ariel.

"Yes," said Nefazia. "I sent home for the fabrics and for the designers. You simply can't find these things in this part of the sea."

"We were very wrong about everything," said Ariel.

"I'm sorry you all misunderstood. You needn't have worried," Nefazia said.

"I think it would be wonderful if you

married Father," Ariel said softly.

"That won't happen," replied Nefazia, gently pushing back Ariel's hair. "But he and I will always be friends. And now I think you and I will be good friends as well."

Ariel hugged Nefazia. "For always!"

"Let's go see your room," Nefazia suggested after a moment. They swam down the hall. "Do you like it?" Nefazia asked as they stood in the doorway.

Ariel was speechless. Her room had been completely repainted. The outer part of the ceiling was a midnight blue, which melted into a deep gold streaked with reds and oranges in the center. The walls were a very light blue green that grew dark near the floor and was gently flecked with gold. The floor itself was a vivid pink.

"It's the sunset over the ocean, isn't it?" Ariel whispered.

Nefazia nodded. She took Ariel's hand and floated with her to the uppermost corner of the room. There, painted in white against the midnight blue, was a small white star. "That's the first star of the evening sky," Nefazia said softly. "A big old blue whale told me it's called the wishing star. Now you'll always have a star to wish on."

"My own star," Ariel sighed. "In my very own sky. Thank you!"

"I want to make the first wish for you," Nefazia said, shutting her eyes. "I wish you a life of adventure and joy. I wish you good friends. And I have a special wish that your restless heart will find what it seeks." She opened her eyes. "That's more than one wish, but then you are a special mermaid, Ariel. Don't ever let anyone tell you differently. I know that great things await you."

Ariel blushed happily. "Do you really think so?"

"I know so," said Nefazia. "If I had a daughter, I would want her to be just like you."

By the end of the week the rooms were finished, and Nefazia was ready to leave. "They're all unbelievably beautiful," said Ariel as she joined her family for lunch in the royal dining hall.

Cook had prepared a special farewell meal for Nefazia. "Seaweed rolls stuffed with plankton paste, with a gentle hint of spicy sea curry," he announced as the waiters set out the huge plates of food.

Everyone tasted the dish. "Wonderful," said Nefazia with a smile.

"I'm starting to like all this spicy stuff," added Aquata.

"That's good," Sebastian said. "Because we now have a cellar full of spices. Cook is all stocked up."

"That means Nefazia *has* to come back soon," Ariel said. "She can't let all those spices go to waste!"

Nefazia smiled at her. "Don't worry. You haven't seen the last of me."

When the meal was finished, Nefazia's staff gathered the rest of her things. She bid King Triton and the mermaids farewell in the courtyard. "Good-bye," she said. "Thank you for having me visit."

"Thank you for our new rooms," said Aquata.

"And for *everything*," Ariel said, giving Nefazia one last hug.

"It has all been my great pleasure," Nefazia told them.

As the grand parade of sea zebras and coaches traveled away, Ariel went up to her new bedroom. "I wish you a safe trip," she whispered, looking up at her tiny wishing star on the wall. "And I wish that when I am grown, I will be just like you."